Blue's Cool Idea

Published by Advance Publishers, L.C.
www.advance-publishers.com

Written by K. Emily Hutta
Art layout by J.J. Smith-Moore
Art composition by Brad McMahon
Produced by Bumpy Slide Books

ISBN: 1-57973-067-1

Hi, there! You're just in time! It's so hot today, and Blue and I could really use your help figuring out how to cool off. Will you help us? You will? Great!

So what do you think we should do? Get out of the sun! Good thinking! Let's go inside, and maybe we can get more ideas for cooling off from some of our friends.

Well, it's cooler in here, but it's still pretty hot. I wonder what else we can do to cool off. You have an idea, Blue? Great! What is it?

Oh! Blue wants us to play Blue's Clues to figure out a good way to cool off. So we'll look for Blue's pawprints on three clues. Are you with me? You are? Great!

You know, cold juice is a smart way to stay cool. I think I'll have some right now. You see a clue? Oh! Orange juice is our first clue!

Wow! Only two more clues to go! In the meantime, let's see if we can find some more ways to stay cool.

Thanks for the tip, Slip! Maybe Blue and I will join you for a dip. What do you think, Blue? Blue? Did you see where Blue went?

Where could Blue have gone? What's that? You wish you knew? Me, too. Oh. Oh! You see a clue! Where? On the art table! Pop sticks are our second clue! Hmmm.

What do you think we can do to cool off using orange juice and pop sticks? Are you thinking what I'm thinking? Yeah. I think we need our third clue before we can figure out the answer to Blue's Clues.

We're looking for ways to cool off, too!
Could you show us how to make paper fans?

Let's see. You fold a paper over and under until it's all folded up like an accordion. Then you hold one end closed and open the other end wide. Hey, I did it! I made a fan! I think I'll wave it back and forth. I feel cooler already! Thanks, Tickety!

Look at my great fan, Blue! Blue? Now where did she go? Let's go find her.

Oh! Hi, Felt Friends! What are you doing to cool off today?

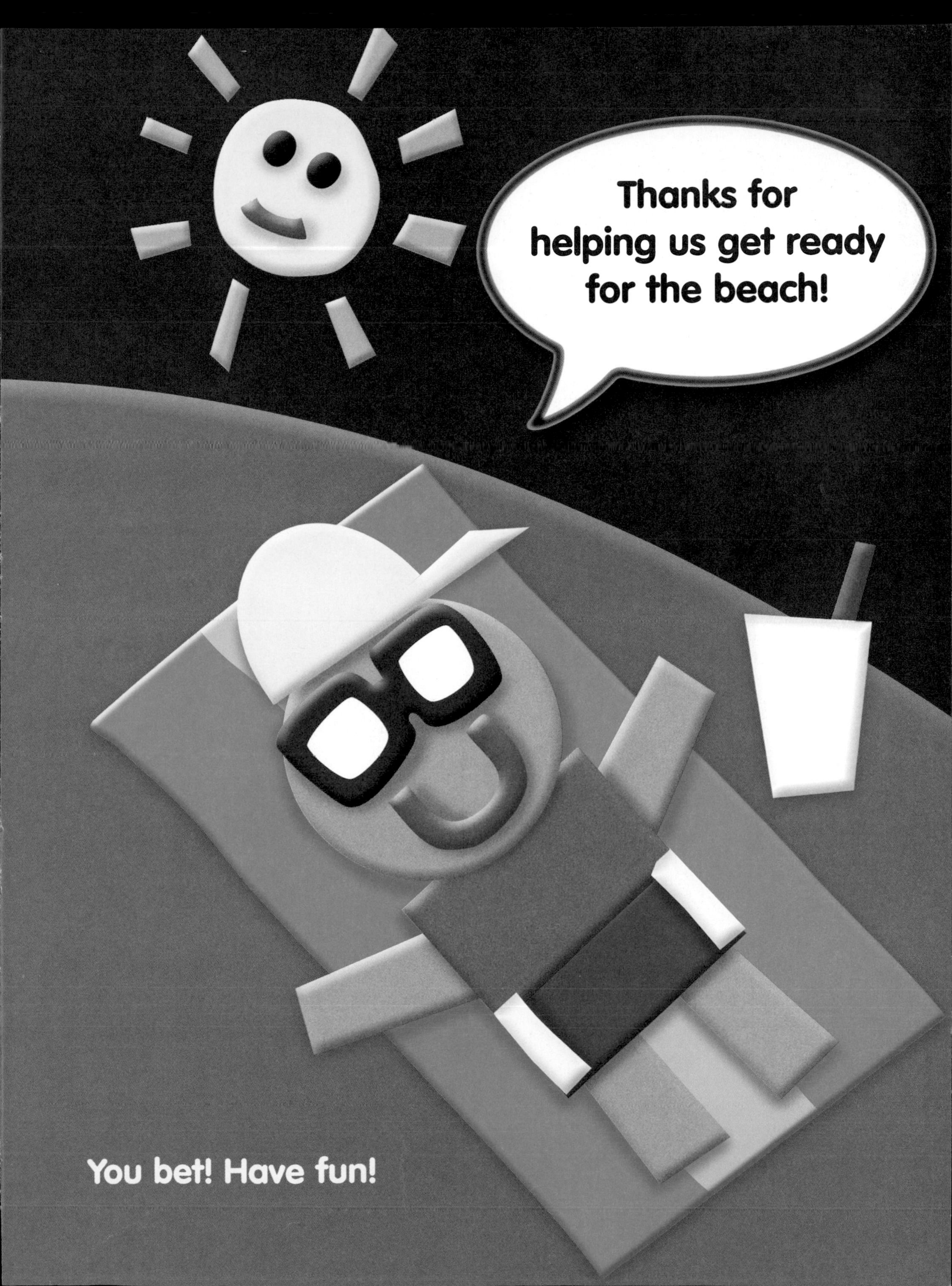

You bet! Have fun!

You see a pawprint? The freezer is a clue. Great job! We have all three clues! You know what that means? It's time to go to our . . . Thinking Chair! Come on!

Okay. Let's think. How does Blue want to cool off with orange juice, pop sticks, and the freezer?

That's it! Blue wants to make frozen juice pops to help us cool down! Great idea, Blue! Let's pop on into the kitchen and make some!

Hi, Mr. Salt, Mrs. Pepper, and Paprika! We're going to make frozen juice pops!

We'd be happy to help you.

Great! We can all work together. We need pop sticks, orange juice, an ice cube tray, and plastic wrap. Now we put the ice cube tray in the freezer until the orange juice freezes. I can't wait for the pops to be ready!

We're back. It's been a couple of hours since we put the orange juice in the freezer. Now our juice pops are frozen and ready to eat! Yum! Thank you so much for your help. You're a very cool friend. Smart, too!

BLUE'S COOL JUICE POPS

You will need: ice cube tray,
juice, pop sticks, freezer, and plastic wrap

1. Get a grown-up to help you pour your favorite juice into an ice cube tray.

2. Put a piece of plastic wrap over the tray (to help the sticks stand up straight).

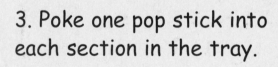

3. Poke one pop stick into each section in the tray.

4. Put the tray in the freezer.

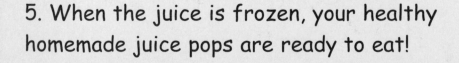

5. When the juice is frozen, your healthy homemade juice pops are ready to eat!